Slimline Tales

Slimline Tales

by Roger Noons

Chapeltown Books

British Library Cataloguing in Publication Data

A Record of this Publication is available from the British Library

ISBN 978-1-910542-27-9

This edition published 2018 by Chapeltown Books
Manchester, England

All Chapeltown books are published on paper derived from sustainable
resources.

For Judy

CONTENTS

ACKNOWLEDGEMENTS

To all those fellow writers in the West Midlands who, during the last ten years have advised and helped me with my writing and in particular Howard Smith, my film making friend who allows me to indulge myself writing his scripts.

INTRO

If you have time to read this volume from cover to cover, that's fine. But if you're limited to dipping, moments here and there to read just a few words, then equally, this slim volume is for you. Each piece has been inspired by something I've seen, heard or been told about. Much of what you will read is based on reality and wherever I have strayed from that, it has been in order to create a story or achieve an appropriate ending.

I have greatly enjoyed writing these brief stories and I hope that you will gain an equal amount of pleasure from reading them. Good luck!

CONVERSATION

"I bet you've had a few women in your time," Jez said after taking the top off a fresh pint of Doom Bar.

"Why do you say that?" I asked, before raising mine to my lips.

"Stands to reason, good-looking chap like you."

I smiled.

"My sister said—"

"What, what did your sister say?"

"That she'd always fancied you and—"

"And?"

"And you were always surrounded by women, at parties. Like peacocks round a buddleia," she said.

"That would be your sister Glenda, the gardener?"

"Yeah, right, how did you know that mate?"

"Intuition," I said, tapping my nose.

THE LADY PHYSIOTHERAPIST

"How did you get on?" his wife asked.

"All right, she gave me a thorough examination, pulled and stretched me, had me turn and twist, touch my toes and do push-ups."

"Do you feel better?"

"No, I feel a damn sight worse. I've not had that much exercise in months."

"Years, more likely," said Helen. "What happens now? Have you to go back to see her?"

"Not unless it gets worse. She's recommended a regime of exercise. I need to concentrate on building up the muscles and strengthen the ligaments in the upper half of my body. Below the waist I'm OK."

"I wouldn't go that far," she grinned.

He ignored her. "I should do the exercises standing up with my feet apart and try not to twist or strain my lower back," Sandy added.

"So, what sort of exercises have you got to do?"

"I need to build up the superficial back muscles, the serratus, deltoid and trapezius, they are wasting at the moment—"

"How will you do that?" queried Helen.

"By moving my shoulders back and forth, raising and lowering the arms. It will also help to build up the biceps, triceps and flexor muscles. In particular, I need to do circular movements of the forearms to strengthen the

Palmaris longus and the Pronator quadratus. Moving the fingers and gripping objects will build up the Radio carpal and metacarpal ligaments. That will strengthen the whole of the upper limbs."

"How often do you need to do these exercises?"

"Three or four times each day," Sandy added.

"Did she say that you had to keep your hands dry?" inquired his wife.

"No, she didn't mention that. Why?"

"Because you can start right away, that regime has a common name," smiled Helen. "It's called washing up."

MARIA

As I paid for my supper at Restaurante O Tapassol for the third night running, Viktor slipped a white card in with my change.

"Maria?" I frowned.

"Yes sir, on her back."

The penny eventually dropped and I turned the card over. *Largo do Socórro,* I read, *No. 13.*

"After ten o' clock sir, brown door, green shutters above. But," he wagged a finger, "not if black Citroen outside. Show the card." He nodded and took away the ceramic dish containing his tip.

The following morning, as it was on my route to visit the church of Santa Maria, which in the past had provided solace and inspiration, I checked out the address. In a clean and tidy area, smelling of disinfectant, the small terraced house stood four doors beyond the Socórro Bar, within twenty five meters of one of Funchal's most significant churches.

Not normally so sensitive, but not wanting Victor to ask if I had visited Maria, I ate at different establishments for the next four evenings. It was on Sunday morning; just after I'd left the hotel that I met him. I felt my cheeks burning as he shook my hand.

"You no go to Maria?"

I shook my head.

"But she expecting you."

Not sure how to explain, I shrugged, but he was in no mood to let me off. His expression demanded a response.

"Er Viktor… I… I don't pay women for sex. I—"

"Who told you sex? Maria is poeta. I see you reading book of poems, I think you should meet."

"All right, I'll go tonight."

He frowned; shook his head. "Ten in the morning, so that little Diogo has gone school."

"Right, I'll go tomorrow, I promise."

We shook hands and parted. After he'd turned the corner, I began to wonder. What was the significance of the black Citroen?

BLACK AS COAL

Samuel Morris was a big man and he had a way with coal. Starting when he was thirteen years old, he found it, dug it, loaded and moved it. He carved it, shined it and burned it. He worked down a mine before the National Coal Board came into existence, in the days when there were no pit head baths. He'd go home and wash himself down as best he could, in a tin bath, or a deep ceramic sink. More often than not using cold water and a lump of green soap cut from a large block.

Unusually for a collier, he did not drink alcohol. He had a reputation for meanness, so it probably grieved him to put money into the pockets of brewers. He did however, drink large quantities of tea, and his great love was gardening. He rented an allotment. Samuel also had a way with vegetables. He would talk to them at length. Spending so much time below ground, he relished the hours with just the sky above him.

Sadly, he did not have a way with God. He boasted that he had entered a church on only three occasions, one wedding and two funerals. In the end the black stuff killed him. Four tons of it fell on him from a small height as he lay on his belly in the cold wet darkness. He was 52 years old and the year was 1941, when he achieved his fourth visit. His widow, Lily, in compensation, was given one hundred pounds, which she spent on a headstone in the cemetery. She also received a ton of coal each year until she died.

LUCKY NUMBER

"And the lucky number is… two hundred and forty, a green ticket."

"Two forty… the Chairman repeated.

"Yes," came a woman's voice.

"That's blue," admonished a neighbour.

"Well someone must have it," murmured the Chairman.

"Draw it again," a man at the back shouted.

"Yes," the Chairman agreed, "draw another ticket."

It seemed to take an age, and there was considerable noise from the packed room.

The woman on the stage brandished a yellow ticket. "Number twelve," she screamed.

"That's me," my ex-wife called out.

"Congratulations Madame, you have won a weekend for two in Paris."

"I've got no-one to go with," she said, staring at me.

PRAYERS

"Right, off to bed with you, and don't forget to say your prayers."

"No Mummy."

Timmy shuddered as he entered his bedroom beneath the eaves of the cottage. He always brushed his teeth, as he did not want them to fall out, but he hated the lingering minty taste.

He drew back the top sheet and underlying blanket, and then knelt, resting his forearms on the sheet-covered mattress. He closed his eyes and leant forward.

"God bless Sam, although he barks too much, and Bobby although he sits on his perch and will not talk to me." He paused; opened his eyes. He swallowed and again closed his eyes, tightly; pressed the palms of his hands together.

"God bless Mummy… and please stop Daddy hurting me."

As he opened his eyes a single tear spilled from each lower lid.

REPORT

"Motor Claims, can I help you?"

"Good afternoon, my name's James Roberts, I have my car insured with your company and I'm afraid I have to report an accident."

"Just a moment Mr Roberts, I'll put you through to…"

"Hello Mr Roberts, my name is Alison; I'll be dealing with your claim. Can you drive it? Are you at the scene?"

"Oh no, I'm at home, it's a bump at the front, on the near side."

"Right, if you give me your policy number, I'll bring up your details to save me asking you a load of questions."

"It's MoI 650089."

"Right, I have the information. If you would like to tell me what happened. If it's straightforward, you may not need to complete a form."

"It was yesterday afternoon, I was driving towards the crossroads at Mossbridge, where the A491 crosses the A4101. I slowed as I neared the shops on my left, but coming towards me was a large 4 x 4 with its lights on main beam. I was dazzled and pressed my foot on what I thought was the brake, but it must have been the accelerator, as I shot forward. There was a jogger, so I swung the wheel, but mounted the pavement and collided with a tree."

"That's it is it?"

"Yes."

"What was she like?"

"Pardon?"

"The jogger, what was she like?"

"How do you know—?"

"Was she wearing tight white shorts, with a pink top? Did she have red hair, a pony tail that bounced from side to side as she ran? Was she wearing Nike trainers?"

"How on earth do you know all—?"

"I'm your principal witness Mr Roberts, but I can't say I remember seeing a 4 x 4 with its headlights on."

ONCE

The clock on the bedside table read 00.17 when the telephone rang. Assuming it would be a reveller calling to wish me Happy New Year, I lifted the handset.

"Hello."

"Look out the window."

"Pardon?"

"Put down the phone, walk over to the window, and look out."

"I don't understand."

"For once in your life, do as you are told."

Shaking my head, I returned the phone to its cradle. Gazing out, I saw nothing until there was a flash. I heard the report followed by breaking glass. I fell backwards on to the bed, and then came darkness.

NOSY

"I hear you're dating that girl from the Central Library?" Ed said.

"Yeah."

"Not that foreign one... Polish is she?"

"No, not that one," Will replied.

"The blonde one?"

"No, the tall one with short dark hair."

"The one with the big—"

"Yes."

"Lucky you—"

"We've only been out a few times... cinema, Macdonald's"

"Yeah, but, she's a bit special... for you... dresses nice, wears high heels. Does she... do you—?"

"What?"

"You know?"

"What?"

"Do you still have to pay fines?"

"Only if I'm late taking my books back."

"Oh."

FINAL CHANCE

It was raining. A fine drizzle illuminated by the warm glow of the street lamp. I had obviously dropped off to sleep and on waking found that the darkness of a November evening had settled. The house seemed quiet. The bedroom door being ajar, I should have been able to hear the sounds of Helena preparing supper; the hum of the radio which she always enjoyed while working in the kitchen.

Then it came back to me. She had left, said I'd had my final chance.

"Fuck it!" I said aloud, and reached for the bottle on the bedside table.

IN PERSON

"Have you thought of banking on line, Mr Lawson?" she asked, as she keyed in the numbers from my card.

"Yes," I stared at her name badge. "Kaye. But if I did so, I would have no excuse to come in every Friday afternoon and enjoy a few minutes in your company."

She looked up, frowning.

"I would not have the delight of your sparkling blue eyes; the joy of your variously painted fingernails, the wonder of your butterfly tattoo, nor the sound of your charming, soprano voice."

She blushed. "How would you like the money, Mr Lawson?"

A LIFETIME OF PAINTING

I came upon him on the river bank; he was sitting facing the cathedral. I looked at his easel and noted that his watercolour was at an advanced stage. I was thrilled by his use of warm tones against the cobalt sky. I stood and watched as he added the final marks with a fine brush, using a rich mix of burnt umber and ultramarine.

After he had put down his brush and contemplated his work, I asked. "How long did it take you to complete?"

"Just under three hours," he said. "Plus sixty three years."

MY HERO

I sat there in the dark. On the spot-lit stage, a stool, a single microphone, a guitar on a stand and a table with a tumbler and a jug of water. I'd waited over forty years for this, after regularly listening to his albums.

"Ladies and gentlemen, please welcome…" I heard no more because of the adrenaline in my bloodstream, the pounding in my ears.

He stumbled on stage, staggered to the microphone and picked up his guitar. From the first chord, he made the instrument sing. The notes burned into my soul and I wept.

SPUR OF THE MOMENT

"I would have thought you were taking a hell of a risk," my mother said, disapproval smeared across her face.

"Why?"

"Accepting an invitation from a stranger on a bus."

"I didn't seem that way to me."

I was settled on the 257 when he got on at the stop that is opposite the old ambulance station. He smiled as he dropped down on the seat opposite, resting his backpack alongside. I resumed my unfocussed gaze through the window. Two stops later, he turned and again smiled.

"Are you up for an adventure?"

I frowned.

"Three stops from now get off with me and I'll take you to the nearest pub and buy you a drink."

I shook my head, in amazement, not in refusal. "And why should I do that?"

"Because it's Friday night and you look like you've had a crappy week and it might cheer you up."

I looked at his boyish smile and the lock of light brown hair that flopped down towards his right eye. "All right," I said, stood up and pressed the bell. "Now," I added and he had to hurry to gather his bag and follow me to the front.

"Which way?" I asked when we were standing on the pavement.
"You choose."

Mum was still shaking her head. "So where did you end up?"

"The Horse and Jockey."

"That dump?"

"It's been done up, new young licensee, they do food now, as well."

"And what did he buy you, half a shandy?"

"Actually, I had a gin and tonic and—"

"Huh, I suppose it's a pound to speak to you now. Although I guess he was looking to get you—"

"Before you ask, I had a second, a double."

"I didn't know you liked gin?"

"It's all right, when someone else is paying."

My mother took a deep breath, loath to celebrate my adventure. "What did you talk about?"

"Films, plays, books, that sort of thing."

"Oh, he's highbrow, is he?"

"He's a teacher, at the Sixth Form College."

"What was he after, that's what I'd like to know."

"He gave me his mobile number."

Her displeasure spanned the five feet between us. "Are you going to ring him?"

I gazed into space. "Probably not."

"I should think not."

"I didn't get around to telling him that I had a three year old child... and a husband in prison for attempted murder."

THAT FRIDAY NIGHT

A unique cabaret, just after ten o'clock on that warm summer's night. All the street came out and the pubs emptied early after a Midland Red bus became wedged beneath the railway bridge, just yards from Cradley station.

"Novice driver mustn't know the route."

"Careered past my window."

"Is anybody hurt?"

"The driver's run away."

Sergeant Bills rubbed all his chins, wondering what to do.

Behind No. 20 Cokeland Place, William Clift, no bus driver but a chain maker by trade, didn't even have a licence, was counting out ten shilling notes.

He enjoyed a wager did Uncle Bill.

ACCIDENT

When Mervyn Davies fell down stairs and broke his neck, his son Philip was not saddened. Many a night he had been awakened by banging on the partition wall between his bedroom and that of his sister. Megan was two years older than Phil; well developed for her fourteen years. He would hear their father's cough as he closed the door, followed by the creak of the floorboards. Pressing his ear against the anaglypta, he would listen to Megan's sobs. It was early on a January morning, when Phil leapt from his doorway, startling his father who lost his balance.

THREES

He realised he was being unfair. He believed she had initially been rude, dismissive, after all, what was it to ask and he had done it politely. It was worthwhile trying to get something knocked off; £25 was a lot to pay for a shirt. Shop assistants had changed he thought, often uninterested; perhaps they were no longer paid commission.

He sighed, resignation reducing his breathing closer to normality. She wasn't to know that he was feeling delicate; fragile, that was the current word. She couldn't know that his wife had again refused him last night; about the threatening letter in this morning's post and... as terrible things were supposed to come in threes, what might happen next.

He strolled aimlessly through the store; found he was approaching *Ladies Underwear* so veered off. The last thing he needed was a hand on his shoulder and accusations of stalking or annoying women when they were choosing lingerie. As he walked on, he heard female voices, loud, discussing intimate details. Glancing to his right, he watched a tall woman carrying an armful of clothing, enter a changing cubicle. His step faltered as she had failed to draw the curtain.

He stared as she pulled up her sweater. Her head and arms were covered, but her bare breasts were free, pointing upwards, nipples protruding. He felt his arousal and hurried from the store, followed the *Toilets* sign. Striding around a corner he halted when his path was blocked by a *Cleaning in Progress* sign. The overalled woman turned towards him.

"I'll only be a couple more minutes love, take a seat."

He dropped down onto a hard, wooden bench. He prayed that this was number three.

SHE

She awoke with a start, though it seemed to take an age to identify the sensations that caused her to hurry to the bathroom. Having emptied her stomach, she splashed cold water on her face, gulped cupped handfuls, and after pushing dampened strands of hair behind her ears, raised her head.

It was her mother's face that stared back from the mirror. Her father's voice which whispered. "I think you've had enough for tonight dear, let's go to bed."

Louise squeezed her eyes shut. Once again she made that silent vow.

SHOPPING

"Are you in ladies underwear?"

I looked the woman up and down. "Err no, not at the moment, I'm—"

"I'm sorry," she smiled. "I thought you worked for M & S."

"No," I replied, I'm standing here between 'push up bras' and the 'T shirt' variety, as my wife's over there buying knickers."

"Oh," she spat, as if I had uttered a four letter word, and strode away. As I stared after her, my wife arrived.

"Was she trying to pick you up?"

"I don't know," I answered. "It's so long since anyone did, I've forgotten what it's like."

"She had so much mascara on her lashes, I'm surprised she had the strength to flutter them."

I stared at Joanne, it was unlike her to be jealous, and show it.

Like most men I guess, I never look forward to visiting a shopping centre, not unless I need socks or perhaps a new shirt. My wife of course, is quite different. There is always something she needs. Makeup, underwear, stationery, a scarf to go with this, a necklace to go with that, and when the new season's fashions arrive, she is eager to look.

"I only want to see what's in for the autumn," she will say quietly.

"Why not choose what you wear according to whether it's warm, cold, dry or wet?" I pose.

"You don't understand."

"No, of course I don't, I'm only a man."

Actually, it's the Dogs Trust that I blame. Every time one of their representatives pushes a plastic bag through our door with FRIDAY writ large on the outside, my wife gratefully accepts the challenge. The reason she 'has nothing to wear', is that most of her clothes have gone to the shop, to pay for bones and doggy chews.

THE PAINTING

Lynne Rogers frowned. "Am I meant to understand what this represents?"

"Mother, don't be such a Philistine!"

"I'm not being anything dear, but having supported you for the last three years and spent thousands of your father's legacy on setting up a studio… it would be nice to know what it is that you've painted."

"It's a collage."

Lynne moved closer to the easel, stared at various parts of the four feet by three feet board. "Is that a dog?" Her finger paused three inches from a blob of either ink or paint.

"It's a hound," Rachel sighed.

"Oh!"

After a further sigh, Rachel lectured, "It represents my feelings about fox hunting."

"I wasn't aware that you had any."

"Precisely."

It was the older woman's turn to frown. "And is it going into your exhibition?"

"Yes."

"Have you decided on a price?"

"Yes… fifteen hundred."

"How much?"

"One thousand five hundred pounds," Rachel stressed, as if addressing a child.

"Does Damian think it will sell?" her mother asked, the chuckle evident in her voice.

"Oh, it's already sold," her daughter casually admitted.

"In that case, you can begin paying rent for the studio, my dear. Shall we say two hundred pounds a week?"

A SUMMER VISIT

The concierge at the hotel suggested I should visit the old monastery.

"It was used as a hospital during the war," he stressed.

"My father fought in the Second World War," I told him.

"Here in Italy?"

"I don't know, all my mother ever said was that he died in a prison camp in Germany."

The slightly-built, uniformed man's face became even sadder. "Perhaps you should not go if it will generate unhappy memories."

I did go however, the following day, and although it proved an arduous climb in the heat, it turned out to be an exquisite experience. The remaining stonework had been absorbed into the arms and bosom of nature; grasses grew in profusion, and all around were masses of yellow and blue flowers, whose perfume though overpowering, brought me peace.

I wondered if I would ever find such a place in Germany.

CALIFORNIAN BELLE

Neither slender, nor slim adequately described the lady; tall, statuesque was more appropriate. Her age carefully disguised, she dominated any gathering. Her manner, in speech, as well as movement, was gentle; a slow drawl to a skater's glide. When playing Trivial Pursuit, she would drive you to distraction. She made you wait, not I believe strategically, but in her desire to prove an adequate opponent. Stylishly-clothed, she never showed too much, or too little, in fact 'middle way' would best describe her; except for her generosity. Without flamboyance, she proved time and again that she was a millionairess.

BUTTERFLY BALLET

A trio of Whites performs a complicated country dance against a shaded fence. A yard away, Peacocks binge on a Buddleia Black Knight bush, on the periphery of which, trips a Comma; low profile, feeding on emerging blooms. A Speckled Wood skips into the garden; nonchalant, ignoring his cousins. If he had the organs, he would surely whistle as he goes along. A Common Blue darts hither and thither, the epitome of fast feeding. Stillness, as the Red Admiral arrives to carry out an inspection, take the salute of the parade. Satisfied, he eventually departs, and normality returns.

CAREER PROSPECTS

Ray Bloomer became a butcher by accident. One Tuesday afternoon, he stood alongside his mother, as she explained to Mr Baxter that she did not have enough money to pay for the meat. Charlie looked them both up and down.

"Your son's a big strong lad. He can come and work for me on a Saturday, washing down, sweeping up, and such like. I'll pay him seven and six."

Mother and son smiled; nodded enthusiastically.

Ray was waiting outside the shop at ten minutes to eight on the following Saturday morning and he left when Charlie said he could go, just after five. He never missed a day and when he left school, Charlie took him on full time. After five years, he qualified as a Master Butcher, and was securely placed when Charlie had a heart attack and died. After a respectable period, Ray married Mrs Baxter.

DANCE WITH ME

The year was one hour and eighteen minutes old when the restaurant door swished shut behind me. The frosty air proved cool and refreshing. As I passed The New Inn, a man and woman exited. The woman staggered towards me.

"Happy New Year, handsome."

I smiled as I heard the man laughing.

She grabbed me; pressed her body against mine. I inhaled a mixture of blackcurrant, sweat and long-applied Opium.

"Dance," she pleaded.

As I hummed the tune of *La Vie En Rose*, we shuffled around on the pavement, once slipping into the gutter.

"Time to go now, Mandy," the man called out.

She planted a hard, wet kiss on my pursed lips, and drew back.

"Bye," she said over her shoulder, leaving me to take my erection home.

DECISION TIME

She was one of the ugliest women I have ever set eyes on, and I've seen a few. At first, I thought it was a man, but the tell-tale signs were there. It wouldn't have been so bad if she'd tried to make the best of herself; if she had done something with her hair; taken professional advice regarding make up, and dressed according to her fifty plus years, rather than like a twenty something.

Helen told me I was being cruel, but what did she expect. There were only six of us; we needed to look our best. If we were going to appear on stage and possibly television, it was all about image; appearance, so at the end of the week, I told her she had to go.

"Oh must I Janet? I have so enjoyed my time with you."

EPITAPH

"… I know I am speaking for all our family, friends and colleagues, when I say what a good man my father was. Indeed, I think the number of people both here in the Crematorium and outside, speaks for itself. Obviously he will be missed…"

Andy kept talking in an attempt to obliterate the sounds of his mother and sister, their sobs echoing around the chapel.

"… In conclusion, I only hope that I can emulate his successes and value to the society in which he lived and worked." As he returned to his seat, he touched Anita's shoulder and having sat, removed his spectacles and dabbed his eyes with his handkerchief.

Relief began after he had led his mother out through the door and into the paved area where the sprays and tributes were displayed. As soon as Anita had joined them, he moved around so that he could acknowledge and thank the many mourners who paraded outside. He recognized a short, stout man, immaculate in a dark suit.

"It's David Clarke isn't it?"

"Yes Andy," the man said, shaking the proffered hand. "I'm sorry about your father, I hope he didn't suffer?"

"No, well not at the end anyway, he was allowed all the morphine he wanted. Actually, you would have known him as well as anybody, much better than most, as he was your boss, for how long?"

"Eighteen years."

"What was he really like, Mr Clarke?"

He studied the lad for some moments, his eyes, slits in concentration. "Honestly?"

"Of course, I wouldn't have asked otherwise."

Clarke shrugged. "He was a bastard… and incompetent with it…"

"Oh!"

EVICTED

What an embarrassment!

I took my grandchildren to the Panto. Alice was a comely wench, but she ultimately led to my downfall. We were encouraged to participate, to call out; hiss and boo. That's what you do – why you go.

It was during the second half, we had enjoyed ice creams; made ourselves comfortable. I was as excited as the kids; made a spectacle of myself. When we were asked to call for the Cheshire Cat, I yelled. "We want Pussy!"

Two burly men marched me out of the Circle, made me wait for Ben and Jack in the foyer.

FAREWELL

The organ played softly, a gentle tune by Bach. Outside, the casket lay on its cradle; a single spray of white and red carnations adorned its top surface. As the mourners arrived, they clustered, speaking quietly in welcome to relatives and friends. A hug here, a kiss or a smile there. At the appointed time, a gaunt man, black top hat in hand, led them into the crematorium. When all were seated, the vicar began to speak.

"Friends, we are gathered here today to…"

I could not hear him. No-one had told me that it was my funeral.

THE SHOP THAT ISN'T THERE

I remember Mary Anne, the proprietress of our local corner shop. You could buy anything there; The Beano, hairnets, a pint of vinegar, a pound of spuds, firewood and if they'd had such things in those days, a toilet roll. She was an innovator; way before her time. She spent long days sitting on three cushions, atop a beech wood box by the till.

"You can help yourself, young man, you know where everything is. Tell me when you're done, I'll tot up your bill."

Her corner shop's long gone; replaced by a self-service store.

HIGH FINANCE

"You know that woman who lives opposite you?"

"Which…?"

"The one who looks like she's got footballs up her jumper. Face like the back end of a bus though…"

"Oh, Elaine?"

"That's her. Do you know she works in the Stockbridge Building Society?"

"Yes, she's…"

"One of the top ones in the branch mate, when she speaks, they jump, I'll tell you. Well she's fixed me up with a mortgage."

"Oh yes, what's the rate?"

"No idea mate, I couldn't take my eyes off her boobs. In fact, I don't even remember signing the form."

INTERVIEW

There was a knock on the door.

"Come in."

"You wanted to see me Mr Rogers?"

"Ah yes, come in Clive, have a seat, would you like a coffee?"

"No, I'm alright… thank you."

"Right, so how's it going? Settling in okay? Got everything you need?"

"Yes, thank you."

"You started on Monday?"

"Last Friday."

"Funny day to start a new job?"

"It was the first of the month."

Rogers glanced at the calendar on his desk.

"Of course… you see, it's right what they say about Gaffers… we really don't know what day it is."

IT DIDN'T MEAN ANYTHING

"Why?"

"What do you mean?"

"Why did you do it, with that woman? I'd just like to understand."

"… I suppose because she offered… it was there on a plate…"

"But why? Don't I satisfy you anymore? What have I done wrong?"

"Nothing," Peter answered quickly, "I still love you and—"

"Well that's a strange way of showing it, going off and screwing a waitress and lying to me, in the hope that I wouldn't find out."

"I didn't want you to find out because I knew you would be hurt."

"Hah!" Susan screamed. "You appreciated that I would be upset, but you still went ahead, you—"

"It didn't mean anything, it was just… a couple of hours in her flat."

"Ah, it was just a quickie, so that doesn't count for anything… let me tell you, it means something to me, and if what I hear is right, it meant something to D—"

"Look, if you're going to get it all out of proportion, there's no point in us discussing—"

"It's a discussion, is it? I don't think so. You have been unfaithful to me, and to cover it up, you told a pack of lies, not only to me, but to your mother as well."

"My mother?"

She stared at him.

"What's my mother got to do with it?"

Susan let out a long sigh. Shaking her head slowly, she said, "who do you think told me?"

J. D. T.

"Cold wind ennet?" the old chap said. He stayed; commandeered the centre of that Wenlock pavement. He shifted his flat cap to the side of his head, over his left ear. "Come for the poetry 'ave you?"

Ignoring my nod, he continued. "You may 'ave 'eard of my uncle, Dylan? I'm John David Thomas, from Shewsbry.

"Of course, he's my favourite… are you a poet?"

He looked up and down the street, I wondered if he had registered my question. I studied him, his thinning white hair; layers of garments at his throat and a neck showing evidence of a lazy razor; waterproof trousers, and highly polished brown boots.

"Are you a poet?" I repeated.

"No, farming," and without further ado, he delivered a twelve minute lecture on how he used to carry out artificial insemination, including the actions, regularly forcing passing pedestrians to step onto the highway.

"When I retired, they often used to invite me to the W.I. meetings."

I didn't dare to ask.

THE WRITER

"What can I get you?"

"A pint of Hobgoblin please."

"I've not seen you in here before."

"I'm with the Priory Writer's group. It's our Annual Dinner."

"Ah, so you're a writer. What are you working on at the moment?"

"A story about a guy who walks into a pub, and the beautiful barmaid instantly falls in love with him, plies him with free drinks."

She carefully places the glass on the bar, looks into his eyes. "And how does it end?"

"I'm not sure; I've not finished it yet."

"Right, well that will be three pounds forty nine please."

MONDAY MORNING

At the bus stop, in last night's make-up, the woman felt her cheeks warm under the schoolboy's stare. He hitched up his backpack, but his eyes never left her face.

"Are you a clown?"

She started, thought to rebuke him, but instead sneaked a glance at her reflection in the graffitied plastic. When she saw the streaked mascara and scratched foundation, she laughed. "I wish I was," she admitted and touched the boy's shoulder, tempted to tousle his hair.

When the bus arrived, she let him get on first. She slipped on her sling backs as he did so.

VISIT

I knew she'd come as soon as she read the message on the card. 'Season's Greetings from Rob.' The absence of 'and Jan' would motivate her to pack a bag and rush to the station.

It was just after seven fifteen, the tail end of Barwick Green was playing, when there was a single ring on the bell. I opened the door and stood aside. She marched in, turned and grinned at me.

'Welcome back."

"I said I'd come as soon as you got rid of that bitch."

"Yes my dear, but how long will you stay this time?"

WARTIME

"Is this your allotment?"

"What's it to you?"

"I am charged with the enforcement of the Defence Regulations. Under Order Number 142b, you are not allowed to grow flowers. Haven't you heard of *Dig For Victory?*"

"These are edible plants," the man with the spade said, and demonstrated by pulling leaves and chewing them.

"They're flowers," he pointed.

"Leaves and flowers that go into soups and salads."

"That's alright then."

"What did he want?"

The gardener laughed. "You'd think they'd send someone who knew the difference between dandelions and nasturtiums."

"It's wartime mate. The blokes with gumption are in France."

MEMORY

"When are you going?"

"Tomorrow."

"Just for the day?"

"No mum, we're staying two nights."

"Have you been before?"

"Yes, lots of times; we go three or four times a year."

"Have I been?"

"Yes, we stopped there once, on the way back from Wales. We had a meal at the Talbot."

"I don't remember."

"I think you do. Dad was with us."

"Oh, you parked in the street, now I remember."

"That's it."

There was silence between us.

"Well I hope you enjoy yourselves; you go while you can. Are you staying the week?"

"No mum, just two nights."

"Going to see that young girl?"

"No, that's in May, when we go to Norfolk to see Rachel, Robert and Fleur."

"How old will she be this time, Furl?"

"She'll be five in July."
"So where are you going this time?"
"To Much Wenlock, for the Poetry Festival."
"For the week?"
"No mum, just Friday 'til Sunday."
"I don't think I've been there, I don't remember it."
More silence.
"So when are you going?"
"Tomorrow."
"Have you told them, in the office?"
"Yes, they know how to contact me, if necessary."
"And where are you going again?"
"To Much Wenlock."
"I don't think I've been there... I don't remember it."
She is ninety-six.

MISFORTUNE

"Come this way miss, gather these moonflowers, use them to mix a potion of love which will attract the richest, most handsome man in the world."

The long-hired, beautiful damsel turned around; stared, but could see no being from whom the breathy words might have emanated.

"Come my lovely, come?"

The maiden moved forward and her nostrils caught the sweet, intoxicating aroma. Without thought, she reached out and plucked the pendulous beauties. She raised her skirt and used it as a trug until it overflowed.

"Come miss, I will guide you so that you might concoct a tincture with which to tempt your hero."

"Sit here my lovely and we will begin."

There appeared beside her on a table, a silver bucket into which she funneled the blooms. Then a silver flask, the contents of which she poured over them. There was a smell of juniper spirit followed by an eruption, a release of dense steam which engulfed her head.

She coughed, retched, grasped her throat until slowly the mist cleared and with it the bucket and the flask. Before her stood a mirror, and when she deemed it safe to open her eyes, she saw the ugliest, foulest creature she had ever encountered.

"Hee, hee, hee," a voice screeched. "You should know my dear; another name for Datura is witches weeds. Welcome to my coven."

Tears streamed from the maiden's eyes, but they were not reflected in the glass.

RISEN

He was an unusual-looking fellow. I would estimate no more than thirty years old. There was not a hair on his head, yet his gingery-grey beard hung halfway towards his broad belt. He wore a black T shirt, bearing in red, the words 'Jesus Has Risen', and as he sat in the airport departure lounge, opposite Gate number 6, he was reading a bible. The last thing I noticed was his sharply-pressed jeans and his heavily scuffed Nike trainers.

A number of his fellow travelers openly stared at him, but he seemed unfazed. On one of the few occasions when he looked up, he would gaze around, smile, slowly stroke his beard, and then go back to his reading. It was not until a message was relayed that the Gate was open for boarding, and he closed his bible and stood up, that I realized he was over six feet tall and weighed probably around eighteen stones.

The strange thing was that when we landed at Gatwick three and a quarter hours later, he was not among the passengers who disembarked.

SIR EDWARD

"He's watching me," Vanessa said.

"Who?"

"That teddy bear on the dressing table, he's watching."

"Ignore him."

"I can't... he looks disapproving... can you turn him towards the wall, or better still..."

I rose from the bed, gathered up Sir Edward and took him into my study. After setting him down on my swivelling chair, I smiled at the old chap. I remembered buying him; we were on holiday in Northumberland. The town where we decided to have lunch had one claim to fame; a teddy bear museum. When we located it, we found a small room alongside a large shop selling a myriad of soft toys.

As our second wedding anniversary was nearing, I invited Jenny to select a bear. She conducted three complete tours and then gathered up a soft, silky-furred, honey-coloured specimen.

"I have different waistcoats," the proprietor announced, "if you wish to change that one."

"No," Jenny said. "Dark brown suits him, makes him look aristocratic."

Just before I turned off the light, a final glance at Sir Edward, he looked disappointed.

When I returned to the bedroom, Vanessa was undressed, reclining on the bed, her contours highlighted by the table lamp. A brief glance confirmed what Sir Edward had meant.

PROSPECTIVE COMMISSION

"Hello?"

"Is that Raymond Fox?"

"Who are you?"

"… You won't know my name, but you were recommended by Jonathan Penn… I hope I'm not disturbing you?"

"I was just touching up a nipple… with a number 2 squirrel."

"Of course you were. What else you would be doing on a Tuesday afternoon?"

"What do you want?"

"Jonathan said you were… adept at dealing with… tricky situations."

"I don't do ceilings."

"Why not?"

"Too much trouble and I've got a bad back."

"I'm not looking at a ceiling."

"What are you looking at?"

"A door, a wall panel, about six feet by four."

"Anything in particular?"

"Elephants, I lived in Africa for a while… and perhaps zebra."

"It's two grand for the door and a hundred quid per square foot for the wall."

"That's a bit steep."

"Well, trompe l'oeil don't come cheap mate."

"When can you start?"

"I'll come and have a look tomorrow, sketch something out and once you've given me the £500 deposit, we can fix a date that's convenient to you."

DIFFICULT DECISION

"Maurice, you have to do something—"

"I can't Mr Bann—"

"Henry please, call me Henry."

"Henry, it's difficult."

"Of course it is, but you cannot carry on like this, you're beginning to spend more time either in hospital or sick at home, than here at the office."

Maurice had lived with his mother until she died, when he was fifty three. His father had been killed in an accident at work when Maurice was eighteen. Four months after his mother's cremation, he married Brenda, who had moved in to care for Mrs Cox during the final months of her suffering from cancer.

He had regularly been shunned by many of his colleagues at Bannan Brothers, where he rose to the position of Chief Clerk and during recent times, had been bullied by his mother and more latterly, his wife.

"You must leave."

"Where could I go? Do they have refuges for battered husbands?"

"You could come and stay with me," Henry said, as he laid his hand on Maurice's wrist.

Maurice looked into the other man's eyes, and believed he recognized gentleness, a welcome, and he too smiled.

WINDOW SHOPPING

She had short fair hair, and though untouched by beauty, her facial expression was one of radiance, as she proudly pushed the buggy along the pavement in the High Street. She paused, gazed in through the window of the Early Learning Centre, enthralled as much by the decorations, the glow and glitter, as she was by the goods displayed. She halted alongside the store offering clothes for children, prominently indicating the age group for which the items were suitable. Smoothing her skirt and pulling around her the worn blue duffle coat, she continued her journey. Regulars smiled as they passed; strangers, after peering into the pram, frowned and shook their heads.

Later, in her bed-sit, lit merely by two advent candles, Alison stared at the television and daydreamed that one day...

THE JOURNEY

When I arrived at Checkpoint Brava, chaos prevailed. I did as directed, parking in a lane for foreigners. I remained in the driving seat. Each time after receiving the signal, I edged forward, until it was my turn. A police officer appeared on each side.

"Papers."

I offered my passport, GDR Entry Visa and the documents relating to the Opel. After what seemed an age, they were passed back, and as the officer gave the signal for the barrier to be raised, his colleague opened the passenger door and jumped in. She squeezed my hand as I accelerated.

TIME TO GO

Samuel halted. The notice on the board screamed EARLY RETIREMENT. He fumbled his spectacles from his top pocket.

"You should go for it," the Foreman said, as he passed by.

He read slowly; a thousand pounds if he volunteered within the week. Trying to remember the current interest rate being paid by the Building Society, he absently selected a piece of French chalk; his arithmetic developed on the brick wall. He turned around, strode towards the stairs and up to the Manager's office.

Twenty minutes later, dazed, he leaned against his bench. "I hope I've done the right thing," he said aloud.

As he walked home, just after five thirty, he was still distracted, almost passing the vicar alongside the lych-gate.

"Mr Lloyd, good evening."

"Oh, sorry Reverend I…"

Another poster attracted Samuel.

"I'm looking for a part time gardener, ten pounds a week?"

"I can start next Monday Vicar," Samuel smiled.

TRIANGLE

"… Don't worry, she has no idea…"

"Are you sure?"

"Certain and I've worked out how I'm going to deal with it."

"What are you going to do?"

"You don't need to know my love, but soon we're going to be together, I promise."

"I hope so."

"I know so… in a few weeks, at this time of night, I'll be undressing you and without needing to hurry. I'll be caressing you, kissing—"

"Oh John, you're making me wet…"

His own arousal was such that he did not register the click.

"John, I think you better ring off or I'll be—"

"Alright my darling, until tomorrow, sleep tight—"

"I love you John."

"Goodnight Agnes my love."

As he walked towards the kitchen, he called, "Usual Chloé?"

Hearing no reply, he stepped through the doorway into the large, attractively furnished sitting room.

"Would you like—?"

The screwdriver was driven upwards into his flesh, pausing only when her wrist was halted by his breastbone. The tip of the ten inch blade pierced his right ventricle. She held the handle until she could no longer support his weight and he fell to the floor. She stared at the stain, surprised as it spread across the material of his blue shirt. The expelled liquid was frothy and although she believed her husband to be dead, there were ugly noises coming from his partly open mouth. The odour of his body's reaction reached her nostrils.

As in a trance, she slowly walked to the telephone on the table alongside the larger of the two sofas. The television was still playing with the sound turned low. She carefully pressed the numbers of her sister's mobile.

"Hello, 077—"

"Agnes I—"

"Chloé?"

"You better come round."

TRIBUTE

Now in her late seventies, she has retained her beauty. Bunned, silky, silver hair; flawless skin untouched by chemicals other than moisturizer, covers majestically-formed bones. A finely proportioned figure, no hour glass, but balanced for poise and bearing. When she enters a room, the eyes of women as well as men follow her. When she smiles, the earth ceases its rotation, if only briefly. Her voice, now a trifle husky, still has enough eloquence and melody to remind me of all those years ago, when I would watch her singing, on a black and white, 12 inch television set.

VIEWPOINT

Matthew, motivated by a desire to have something about which to boast to his fellow pupils, climbed the ladder left against the wall by his next door neighbour. Mr Chrimes had been painting the fascia for several days. He had taken so long, Matthew calculated, because his vantage point offered a view into a bedroom at number 22 Beech Crescent. As he neared the top, wondering which of the dwelling's female occupants he might witness, his mouth fell open. Through the window, he saw Mrs Beverley, being embraced by a man. When the man turned, he identified his father.

ENGLISH

"Are you English?"

"British… yes."

"Er, that's what I meant… you speak English?"

"As a native."

She stared; perhaps she had made a mistake, but he was good looking and appeared confident and well off.

"Is it your first visit to Puerto de Soller?" she asked, "I'm assuming you don't live here."

He smiled, which consoled her.

"No, I come every year, spend most of June here… and you, have you been before?"

"Yes, but it was some years ago, before all this was done." She used her arm to confirm that she was referring to the development of the esplanade and pedestrianised areas.

"Yes, it has made a big difference."

A waiter appeared. "Si señor?"

"Would you care for a drink?" he asked.

"Oh, thank you, that's kind, a fizzy water please?"

"It is after twelve…"

"In that case, a dry white wine would be nice."

"Un vaso de vino blanco, y una cana, por favor."

"Si Señor."

And that was how they had met.

Two drinks segued into lunch which was accompanied by a bottle of rosado, so by three o' clock they were both a little tipsy and laughed as much as they chattered about any nonsense which came to mind. They had coffee, after which he asked for the bill. When it came and he reached to pluck it from the table, she placed her hand on his.

"We should share the cost."

"Why?"

"Well… because I don't want you to get the wrong idea about me, that I'm—"

"Perhaps you will permit me to be a gentleman on this occasion… and… perhaps tomorrow, you can pay?"

"Right," she said, "it's a date."

And that was how they came to meet again.

FOOTBALL RESULTS

My mother was a trained dressmaker and tailoress. During the War, when either she, or one of our neighbours, could acquire a remnant of material, she would run up a blouse, sometimes a skirt. She would also create the pattern using newspaper. I would sit in the corner of our living room playing with whichever toy was my current favourite. On a Sunday afternoon, after my father had come home from work, he would sneak a look at Nellie Cotton's bosom and smirk, as he read Arsenal 2 Portsmouth 3, on the front page of the Sports Argus.

SHOWER

It was not a real thunderstorm, more of a shower, but being on Formby beach on my way back from photographing red squirrels, I still got soaked to the skin.

As soon as the rain stopped, the sun appeared and the north westerly wind, I believed, would aid the drying of my clothes. I was wrong. When I arrived back at the boarding house, I still had the appearance of a submerged Rattus Norvegicus.

"Good gracious me," Mrs Lloyd said, "I didn't know it was raining," as she ushered me in through the front door.

"I got caught on the beach," I admitted, feeling sorry for myself.

"Never mind, get yourself upstairs, there's lots of hot water, have a good soak in the bath. I'll bring some towels."

It was almost half an hour later when the door opened.

"How're you feeling now?" my landlady asked. "Ready to be dried off?"

I often remember that day in Formby. One of my pictures won a hundred pounds in a Nature Photography competition.

SICK LEAVE

"He's off sick."

"Who, Philip?"

"Yeah, he—"

"What's the matter with him?"

"Stress."

"Stress? What's he got to be stressed about?"

"Dunno—"

"The only time he ever gets stressed is at the end of the month, worrying how to get his flexi day in."

"Well, he's got a note... for a month."

"A month? Who's supposed to cover for him, for a month?"

Alan shrugged. "We are, I suppose."

"Well he's got no chance, I can tell you."

"No work to do chaps?" Neither Alan nor Mike had heard Mr Bingham enter the room.

"Is that right Gaffer, about Philip?"

"Yes, apparently he's quite ill, so his wife tells me. He can't sleep, can't eat—"

"Can he fish?"

"Pardon?"

"Fishing, I saw him along the canal on Sunday."

"Good for stress, fishing," Alan chipped in.

Mr Bingham walked from the room, shaking his head.

"I suppose Phil will be back tomorrow?"

Alan looked up. "Apparently, he's sent in another note."

"What!" Mike exclaimed. "We've got to cover for another month? I'm not having that." He stood up. "I'm going to see Bingham."

"Is that right Mr Bingham," Mike began, one foot through the door. "We've got to cover for Philip for another month?"

The manager's hands were bridged, his fingertips touching his chin. "I'm afraid it will be longer than that Michael. His body was recovered from the canal at six thirty this morning."

SOPHIE'S STORY

The Judge ignored my barrister's mitigation, said I was heartless, killing the father of my son. She sentenced me to ten years in prison. Simon was born four months later. He was premature, not expected to live. He was in the hospital for just over a year, and then I got to hold him, spend time with him. I never took him to my breast as by that time, I'd dried up. He was wrinkled and weak. I was allowed to have him for two hours each day. He died yesterday, all alone. He never saw the sky.

A LA CARTE

"That's what comes of trusting the Merc's Sat. Nav.," she declared, as she flounced into the restaurant. Standing in the doorway, she surveyed the scene as she unwound her seemingly endless scarf. "We should have come in my BM," she announced.

"For God's sake, get out of the way Anna, we all want to come in out of the rain."

Still unmoving, Anna smiled sweetly as the young waitress approached.

"Do you have a reservation?"

"Templeman, for five," Anna said, and stepped towards the bar to which the girl had turned to check the diary.

"Ah, yes, one o'clock—"

"Well, as I said, you need to blame Mercedes… and my husband's driving, of course."

"We're sorry to be late, my dear," the bald-headed man smiled, as he swerved around his wife. He didn't see Anna's withering look as they were led to a round table in the far corner.

"If you'd like to check the amount and put in your pin number, Mr Templeman, I—"

As the waitress looked away, Mrs Templeman chipped in, "Don't forget what I said my dear, don't waste your money on a Merc."

"No, I won't Madam, I'll stick with my little Fiat." She turned away. "Thank you Mr Templeman. I hope everything was as you expected? Oh, thank you sir."

When the waitress looked, she saw that he had given her a ten pound note, to accompany his weak smile. Her reverie was disturbed as the door banged shut. She could still hear the woman's voice.

"I hope it's going to get us home, William, perhaps—"

AWARENESS

"Anyway, I told her that no way was I going to—"

"Hey, turn that thing off, are you blind? There's a sign up there," I pointed.

"She's a stuck up bitch, I'm—"

"Turn off that phone or I'll stick it up your arse and you'll only be able to make internal calls."

"It's some bloke who… Who do you think you're talking to?"

I stood up and although I'm the wrong side of seventy, I don't look it, and being six feet two and seventeen stone, people tend to take notice of me. As I moved forwards he ran along the carriage. I smelled his fear as he pulled at the door and his relief when he realised it was sliding, and he managed to open it.

As I returned to my seat, I heard murmured and whispered 'thanks' and 'well done.' It was quiet after I sat down and re-opened my book. '… *yes Pooh, answered Piglet…*'

SWAN SONG

One of my father's last wishes was that his ashes be strewn onto the River Severn, where he had often cast his fishing line. I carried out his wish, accompanied by my mother, on an afternoon in October. I stood on the riverbank about ten feet above the water, and after murmuring a few words, and receiving a nod from my mother, launched the remains. As I did so, a swan paddled towards me. In seconds the white plumage had turned grey, and we watched open-mouthed, as my father traveled on his final journey downstream towards Bewdley Bridge.

BEAUTIFUL MORNING

It is a beautiful morning, the best so far this year. As I gaze out through the kitchen window, the garden looks splendid. There is yellow, red and blue in every bed and all signs of winter are either gone, or well covered. The shrubs at the bottom have come into leaf and obliterated the fence. As I look down, sunlight glints on the brillo pad; a circular rainbow appears on each globe in the washing up bowl.

"Have you nearly finished?" a voice warbles from the hallway.

"Yes dear."

I always believe in having the last word.

COMPANIONS

He walks the streets, the old man, in wind and rain, seven days a week. Overcoat to his ankles, cap pulled down over his eyebrows, jaw jutting forward, he leads his faithful mongrel; half Labrador, half sheep. He is well known on the Estate, always smiles when greeted by neighbours, touches his cap to ladies, but never speaks and his companion never barks. Albert lost his tongue to cancer ten years previously and Rover remains silent in sympathy. His home help tells anyone who will listen. "You can bet that when one of 'em goes, the other will quickly follow."

DISREGARD

She had told him in no uncertain terms. "If you come back here, I'll kill you."

Having watched the house for over an hour, he judged she was alone, so made his way swiftly to the back door. The garden at the side was tidier than when he was responsible, he noted. *I assume I've been replaced.*

Without knocking, he opened the door and stepped inside. Hearing a sound, he turned and the iron bar crashed onto his head. As he lay on the tiled floor, blood pooling alongside his cheek, he smiled. *Better this than endless years inside.*

HOT DATE

"Your mother tells me you're going out tonight?"

"Yes, we're going to see *Lady Windermere's Fan* at the Theatre Royal."

"The man who's taking you—"

"Brian, yes?"

"What's he like?"

"Usual, one head, a torso, two arms, two legs, although I've not actually seen his legs—"

"That's not what I meant—"

"Dad, I'm thirty two."

"Yes, I know but… are his intentions… honourable?"

"I bloody well hope not, otherwise I've wasted seventy quid on a revealing fuchsia silk top and another fifty on slinky black pants."

"You're surely not going to the theatre in trousers?"

GUILTY

The man sat impassively while the third woman described how he had imposed his will, against her wishes. He smiled inwardly. Many eyes had turned towards him when, encouraged by Counsel, she described how well-endowed he was. Before she could be stopped, she mitigated that he had not been cruel; had not hurt her. After he heard reporters rushing from the Court, he made up his mind. The following day, he would change his plea. After how he had been described, he had no wish to announce that during seventy two years he had never once experienced arousal.

CHANGE

I turned the corner and saw the beggar sitting on the pavement outside the pedestrian's entrance to the car park. As I neared, I could see the usual hunched, woolly-hatted man, but rather than the expected RSC-trained mongrel, he was accompanied by a pure white Staffie. I say white, but as I drew level, I noticed a black smudge over her right eye, as if she had applied eyebrow pencil in a hurry and been interrupted before doing the other one.

"Can you—"

"Sorry, I don't give—"

"Can you change this?" His hand thrust forward; contained a ten pound note.

I stared.

"I need coins. If I try to spend this, they'll think I've nicked it."

I realized he was absolutely right. As we looked into each other's eyes, he could obviously read my mind.

"A woman came past, ten minutes back, on her way from the bookie's, she said. Black, she was, singing. She peeled a note off a roll and give it to me."

I nodded and withdrew a plastic bag from my trouser pocket. My see-through purse, I call it. A quick calculation suggested about six pounds. I handed the bag to him.

"Keep the note," I said. "Ask the next guy who comes along."

He smiled and patted the dog's head.

I was still feeling warm and happy ten minutes later, when I turned off the island into the hospital's grounds. It dawned on me that I had no change for the car park, so I drove around and returned to the highway. It was just over half a mile before I found a place to park in the street.

DEPARTURE

"Do you have to go today?"

"Well, I said I would."

"Another couple of days wouldn't... said? Who did you say it to?"

He turned away; she sensed he was fiddling with his man bag.

"You said there was no-one else—"

"There isn't... Oh, Bev, please don't make this any more difficult than it is, I—"

"Robert, it's not me who announces on Christmas Eve that he cannot bear to spend a minute longer in my presence. It's not me who has been surreptitiously removing clothing and possessions from the marital home. I've not suddenly decided to kick twenty years of what I believed to be a loving relationship, into the long grass." She ceased, as she had run out of breath.

Calmed, she asked quietly. "Who did you say it to, someone at work, your mother, who?"

He walked from the kitchen, stood in the hallway staring at the tree, seemingly observing the lights and decorations for the first time. She followed him.

"There is someone else, isn't there?"

His shoulders sagged, he slowly turned, raised his head, looked into her eyes. "I didn't want to hurt you, I didn't want you to..." He paused when he saw the reflected red and green on the blade of the chef's knife; one of the gifts he had bought her for Christmas the previous year. "Bev, don't do anything—"

She thrust her arm forward, felt the pain as far as her shoulder, but the blade deflected, plunged into flesh and a spurt of blood hit her cheek. She snatched back her hand as if the handle had been hot. Staring down at him, watching his blood seep into the carpet, she spat.

"You wanted to go, you bastard, so go."

TELL ME

"You ask me if I love you.... I would have thought it would have been obvious. I work all hours God sends, sweat buckets to achieve top bonus, and hardly spend anything on myself. When I'm here, I'm either working in the garden, cleaning cars, or doing jobs around the house. I added the conservatory you asked for, and next week I'll start on the built-in wardrobes. What more do you want?"

"For you to tell me."

"What?"

"For you to say it, at least once each day, say "Jan I love you."

"Oh, is that all?"

THE END

I studied him, his gait, his manner, his behaviour, and he returned my stare. They came for him, led him inside, I heard his final sounds. The gate closing and the firing of the gun. Later, I squeezed his lungs, plunged my knife into his heart, stabbed at the liver. I turned my attention to his body, by now a mere carcass. Skinned, it was red raw, still twitching as it hung in the cool hall. Finally, the head. I'd been a Meat Inspector at the abattoir for two years, but the head was still the worst part.

GEORGE SMITH

I went to his funeral, although I never knew him. Lots of nice things were said about George Smith, he was obviously well liked, loved even. The front row at the crematorium was taken up by his two sons and their wives. Not one of them wore black, but each shed a tear when his business partner of over thirty years spoke about his life. He had been successful and generous towards those less well off. He had regularly supported local and national charities; given away millions of pounds.

When my mother had seen the announcement in the local newspaper, she told me that he was my father. It was a one night stand apparently, a twenty first birthday party. He was kind, gentle with her, it was her first time. She never told him she had conceived. She said I have his eyes. I wish I had some of his money.

JANUARY

It was the coldest January anyone could remember. For weeks the canal had been frozen.

My father had planted the back garden with vegetables, but the hard ground made it difficult to dig them up. I took a saucepan of boiled water to gather a few sprouts. A week of warm, watery soup, constantly hovering over the range, and the three of us bickered from morning to night.

On Friday morning, my brother left for work, general dog's body at The Chainmakers Arms.

Eight hours later, as it was getting dark, there was a knock on the back door.

"Is Mr Fellows in?"

"No," I said to the Sergeant.

He rubbed his chin. "Are you Sadie?"

I nodded.

"Tell your dad Jimmy's in the cells. He'd best come to the station."

"What's he done?"

"Stolen bread and no doubt other stuff."

I closed the door, and smiled.

When dad returned, he emptied his bag of four lumps of coal and a dozen pieces of firewood.

"You didn't steal it? 'Cause Jim's already at the Police Station."

He shook his head.

"You bank the fire up; I've got to nip out," I told him.

There were no lights at the pub, so I crept around the back. Wedged behind the two old barrels, I found the bag.

As we ate our supper of crusty bread, corned beef and pickled onions, I asked if he were going to the Station.

"No, I'll go tomorrow, the Sergeant'll likely smell my breath.

LIKE A SHOT

"Norris!"

"Yes sir?"

"What are you doing on Saturday?"

"Nothing in particular sir."

"Yes you are. You're in the school team for the District Sports; it's at Bromsgrove. Be here at nine o' clock, I'll take you."

"In which event sir?"

"Er… discus… and shot of course."

"Right oh sir."

He glared; my expression obviously came within his definition of 'familiarity.'

Saturday arrived, and I stood at the bus stop with my bag.

"Do you have to go on a Saturday now Ralph?"

"No Mrs Wyre, I'm in the school team for the District Sports."

"That sounds grand!"

I nodded, smiled, and stood back to let her get on the bus.

"Good luck!" she shouted, as I climbed the stairs.

At ten minutes past four in the afternoon, I was awaiting the 137 to return home, when our neighbour waddled towards me. She was festooned with shopping bags; her husband's old haversack over her right shoulder.

"Hello young 'un," she grinned.

"You're loaded down Mrs Wyre, let me help you."

"Been to the market, haven't I, stocked up with clothes and things for our holiday. We're off to Weston next Saturday."

While I was considering a response, she leaned towards me. "How did you get on then?"

"Fourth," I answered, "in the discus."

"That sounds good, out of how many?"

"Fourteen schools I think."

"Very good!"

"I came second in the shot putt."

"Is that where they throw them canon ball things?"

"Yes," I smiled.

"You want to watch you don't drop it on your foot!"

The bus stopped with a squeal of brakes. I stayed back, then followed her along the lower deck, limping.

RACHEL

"Are you Rachel?"

"Only on Saturday nights, dear. The rest of the week, I'm Raymond and I don't always shave every day."

"My brother said you would probably help me."

"What would a pretty young thing like you want from an old queen?"

"I'd like to get into the theatre."

"Just buy a ticket, dear."

She laughed. "My brother's Gordon Le—"

"In that case, give me your number, I'll make a few calls and ring you. What's your name?"

"Steve, on Saturday nights, otherwise I'm Susie."

Ray stared. *What a waste,* he thought, as she handed him her card.

THE PHOTOGRAPHER

Dawn begins its mellowing of the landscape. The tree skeletons stride forward. Their contours sharpen and their reflections appear darkly in the silent, still, pale grey water. The photographer stands and puts his eye to the viewfinder. Satisfied with the composition, he points his light meter at a mid-tone area in the foreground. He adjusts the aperture ring on the lens, deciding on f11. Unconcerned about the shutter speed, as any slight movement will add to the quality and creativity of the captured image, he gently squeezes the shutter release.

One hour later, having sated his monochrome appetite, he carefully packs away his equipment. He's impatient to return to his studio, yearning with a long maintained energy to closet himself in his darkroom. He is hungry to develop and fix his film, anxious to view his negatives and produce a contact sheet. Once satisfied with his arrested images, he will relax, take a break and replenish his energy with a substantial breakfast.

The contentment proves temporary and two hours later he is back in the windowless room. The equipment is suffused with a dull, flat, red light of such low intensity that many objects are rendered unclear by shadow. His knowledge of the layout is such that he could operate in total darkness, but the safelight renders his occupation less lonely. He talks to himself in mantra to avoid forgetting some part of the standard process.

Six hours later, exhausted, he sits, smiling, in his study; on the desk before him, a selection of ten by eight glossy prints. The pictures charm him with their beauty, their quality and mood. They delight him with the knowledge that he is still as good a photographer as he was all those years ago.

Today is his 85th birthday.

EXPERIENCE

Outside the rain has stopped. A pigeon coos on the windowsill. It puffs up its body, marches back and forth, and takes flight.

I had once believed I could fly. The day following my sixth birthday, I leapt from my bedroom window. It proved a painful, but valuable lesson. The broken arm soon mended and the scar on my forehead has often opened a conversation. During my teenage years it regularly elicited sympathy from caring young ladies.

The lesson I learned on that Thursday morning, was that you did not have to try everything yourself; you could learn from the experience of others. Trust the veracity of their actions. I have to say however, that I have never had much faith in what I read in books or saw in photographs.

My mother always stressed the value of honesty, of treating others as you would have them treat you. She was kind, caring, often put others first. Where did it get her? Little further than where she began.

I also learned that others could be persuaded to experiment on your behalf. Since my seventeenth birthday, when I left home, I have only ever taken one risk. By careful thought and a lack of greed, I have always found others to act for me.

My one mistake was trusting a woman who confessed her love for me, promised forever, if I would just carry out a single task.

The pigeon has returned, the metallic sheen around its throat reflecting through the window. I glower and it stares back, head on one side, aware that the steel bars are on my side of the glass.

FOREGONE CONCLUSION

It happened exactly as I expected. I knew it would, but I still had to laugh.

I was sitting on the terrace of the Grand Hotel, Tremezzo, a dish of almonds and a glass of prosecco at my right hand. As a change from gazing at the lake, its boat traffic, the towns and villages opposite and the mountains beyond, I cast my eyes down to the hotel's swimming pool. A rectangle of rich blue, floating in the greenish water that was Lake Como.

I watched two boys, perhaps brothers, walk along the pontoon. They were wearing the latest designer 'long' shorts and dragging the hotel's towels on the slatted walkway. The taller boy, eight or nine years old, I would guess, was leading the younger one, his arm around the shorter boy's shoulders.

They arrived at the pool's surround, and finding no furniture, deposited the towels on the boards. The taller lad took his brother's hand, seemingly to lead him to the pool's edge. Junior was hesitant; he held back. Big boy obviously decided that persuasion would be the best policy. He again rested his arm on the younger boy's shoulders and began pointing and arguing in favour of them walking to the edge, and together, holding hands, leaping into the blue.

Junior needed much coaxing, but his brother was patient and eventually appeared to win the argument. They moved forward and senior, thinking he had won the day, grabbed his brother's hand and sought to launch him into the pool.

Shorty however, was not born yesterday. He slipped his brother's grip and the taller boy's momentum took him forward and into the water. Although I was 35 meters distant, I heard the plunge, saw senior splashing and spluttering and could see junior's joy in his body language.

It took me back sixty years, when a similar thing happened to me, and I have to tell you that I was not the junior.

Also By Chapeltown Books

From Light to Dark and Back Again
by Allison Symes

This is a collection of flash fiction pieces. The tones vary from humorous to dark and back again but all reflect Allison's style of fiction. Some have appeared on Cafélit (http://cafelit.co.uk) and others on Shortbread Short Stories. The latter are some of the very first pieces she wrote years ago, Cafélit is more recent and other stories are brand new for this collection.

Order from Amazon:

ISBN: 978-1-910542-06-4 (paperback)
978-1-910542-07-1 (ebook)

Chapeltown Books

January Stones
by Gill James

These stories were written one a day throughout January 2013. They were originally published on a blog called Gill's January Stones. Sometimes the stories would come right at the beginning of the day. Sometimes they would take a while longer.

Do they have a theme? Not really, though the idea of 'stones' is one of turning them over slowly on the beach until we find the right one.

There was no strict word count. Each story is as long as it needs to be. It had to be finished, though, by midnight of that day.

Order from Amazon:

ISBN: 978-1-910542-10-1 (paperback)
978-1-910542-11-8 (ebook)

Chapeltown Books

Spectrum
by Christopher Bowles

A collection of one hundred and ten pieces of flash-fiction and poetry. You probably won't like all of them, and some of them might even disgust you, or make you uncomfortable. But stick with it. Look at overarching themes within each coloured block. Find the puns in certain titles. Research the colours that you've never heard of. Try and work out which stories are complete fabrications, which ones contain nuggets of truth, and which ones are versions of real life events.

Order from Amazon:

ISBN: 978-1-910542-13-2 (paperback)
978-1-910542-14-9 (ebook)

Chapeltown Books

www.ingramcontent.com/pod-product-compliance
Lightning Source LLC
Chambersburg PA
CBHW081210170626
46811CB00010B/3234